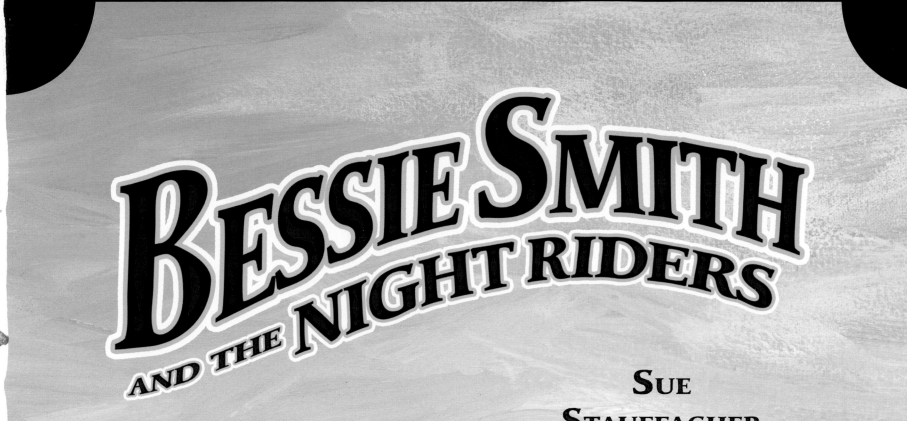

BESSIE SMITH
AND THE NIGHT RIDERS

SUE STAUFFACHER

ILLUSTRATED BY
JOHN HOLYFIELD

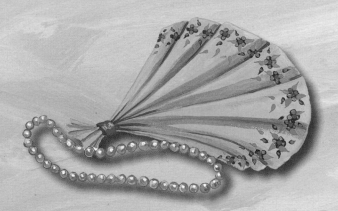

G. P. PUTNAM'S SONS

It seemed like the whole town of Concord held its breath the day Bessie Smith rolled into the station. Bessie was the most famous blues singer in all the South, maybe even the whole world.

I wanted to be the very first to see Bessie's train car, the one made special just for her. Folks said it was twice as big and three times as fine as the one the rich folks rode in from Atlanta.

And there it was, cutting through the dust. Then, just like a dream, Bessie swung off the top step in a red dress and a feather boa.

She looked us over and sang like her heart
was breaking.

I've got the blues, I feel so lonely
I'll give the world if I could only
Make you understand
It surely would be grand . . .

Flicking her feather boa over her shoulder, she
shouted to the crowd, "It surely would be grand
to see every one of y'all tonight at the show."
I pressed my hands to my hot cheeks. Folks poked
me, stepped on my feet, but I didn't feel a thing except
Bessie's words wrapping themselves around me.

Oh, I had a powerful urge to see Bessie sing that night.
But a girl needed shoes, a Sunday dress, and change in
her pocket to see the Empress of the Blues—no, Bessie
wouldn't sing to raggedy ole Emmarene Johnson.

Bessie and her troupe set up their tent on the
edge of town. That night, I hid myself in the
woods and watched as every single ticket
was sold.

When the last man crushed his cigar in the dirt and went inside, I snuck right up close. And when I was sure no one was looking, I pulled back the tent flap for just one peek.

The band was taking the stage. Men practically jumped out of their seats to get the first look.

And there she was, waving that feather boa and singing "Whoa, Tillie, Take Your Time." You might not think the crowd would fancy a gal as big as Bessie, but when she came on stage in her sequined dress and her strings of pretty pearls, every eye was on Bessie Smith.

That band could play something fierce and Bessie belted out one song after the other: "Gimme a Pigfoot," "Lady Luck Blues," "You Don't Understand," and "Ticket Agent, Ease Your Window Down."

Just as she finished singing "I'm out here for
trouble, I've got the Black Mountain blues," I heard
a strange sound outside.

I peeked around the side of the tent and waited
for my eyes to get used to the darkness. That's when
I saw 'em, two figures covered in white sheets working
tent stakes out of the earth.

The Night Riders had come for Bessie!

I shook my head to get my thinking straight. Only one thing Night Riders were good for, and that was trouble. Somebody had to warn Bessie.

I ran past the lanterns at the entrance to the tent and rushed toward the stage. The music stopped.

"It's the Night Riders, Bessie," I managed to gasp.

Some folks run from trouble. Not Bessie. She headed right past me and toward the opening of the tent.

When we stepped outside, we saw that a dozen men on horseback had joined the other two. They held their torches high and stared at Bessie.

"Y'all best get ready to meet your maker," a voice shouted out. That's when I realized those men were planning to burn Bessie's tent to the ground with all those black folks inside.

That didn't sit too well with Bessie. She started cussing up a blue streak.

"You just pick up them sheets and run," she hollered, "if you know what's good for you!"

But then, she seemed to understand this called for more than shouting. So she stopped all that and stood still for a minute.

She started flapping her arms real slow. And she gave one of those low moans she was so famous for, a moan that said, "I may be down and out, but I ain't gonna take it no more."

Her dress shimmered in the light of all that fire as she ran toward the Night Riders. Folks said afterward Bessie looked like a pearly-bright phoenix bird rising up to the Promised Land.

I bet those horses never seen anything like Bessie that night.
The lead man's horse reared right up. His torch grazed the poor
animal's behind and set it off like a firecracker, straight into the line
of horses. They bolted, too. Other torches got dropped. A couple of
sheets caught fire. By then, the Klansmen were yelping up a storm as they
took off, back to the woods.

It was a right funny sight, but nobody laughed. No, Bessie, she stood still,
breathing heavy. She waited a long while, looking up at the stars.

Finally, she turned around, walked straight up
to me, and took my hand. Bessie led me to a seat
in front.

The audience was still in some shock, so Bessie's
first job was to put some backbone in 'em. She
sang "'Taint Nobody's Bizness," and "I Ain't
Gonna Play No Second Fiddle."

And then they clapped and they shouted. Because she drew the trouble from their souls with her big voice, and sent those troubles flying over the treetops, free on the night air.

No, sir, I'll never forget the night that Bessie Smith scared off the Night Riders. That was the night I learned you can look the devil in the eye and spit on the ground. That was the night I decided that if Bessie Smith wasn't gonna take no mess, then neither was Emmarene Johnson.